Fall of the House of Mandible

Don't miss the other spine-tingling
Secrets of Dripping Fang adventures!

SECRETS OF
DRIPPING FANG

BOOK ONE:
The Onts

BOOK TWO:
Treachery and Betrayal at Jolly Days

BOOK THREE:
The Vampire's Curse

SECRETS OF
DRIPPING FANG

BOOK FOUR

Fall of the House
of Mandible

DAN GREENBURG

Illustrations by SCOTT M. FISCHER

HARCOURT, INC.

Orlando   Austin   New York   San Diego   Toronto   London

I want to thank my editor, Allyn Johnston, for her macabre yet soulful
sense of humor, for her eagerness to explore ideas beyond the bounds of taste,
for understanding an author's poignant thirst for praise, and for helping
me say exactly what I'm trying to say, except more gooder.
I also want to thank Scott M. Fischer,
an artist with dizzying technical abilities and a demented genius
at combining terror and humor in the same illustration.
—D. G.

Text copyright © 2006 by Dan Greenburg
Illustrations copyright © 2006 by Scott M. Fischer

www.HarcourtBooks.com

Library of Congress Cataloging-in-Publication Data
Greenburg, Dan.
Secrets of Dripping Fang. Book four, Fall of the House of Mandible/
Dan Greenburg; illustrations by Scott M. Fischer.
p. cm.
Summary: After the Mandible sisters kidnap his sister Cheyenne,
Wally seeks the help of a group of orphans and his vampire father.
[1. Brothers and sisters—Fiction. 2. Twins—Fiction. 3. Ants—Fiction.
4. Vampires—Fiction. 5. Cincinnati (Ohio)—Fiction.] I. Title: Fall of
the House of Mandible. II. Fischer, Scott M., ill. III. Title.
PZ7.G8278See 2006
[Fic]—dc22 2005022603
ISBN-13: 978-0-15-205475-5 ISBN-10: 0-15-205475-8

Text set in Meridien
Designed by Linda Lockowitz

First edition
A C E G H F D B

Printed in the United States of America

For Judith and Zack
with spooky love

—D. G.

Contents

Fall of the House
of Mandible

CHAPTER 1

The No Child Left Alive Program

"Let me tell you how much I hate human children," said Dagmar Mandible to her sister, Hedy.

Dagmar gazed down the row of waxy green cornstalks where the Shluffmuffin twins had vanished and cursed softly under her breath. Nourished by the gentle Cincinnati rains, this year's cornstalks grew higher, bushier, and more lushly than those in the rain forest, assuming that corn grows in the rain forest, a shaky assumption at best.

"No, *hate* is too weak a word," said Dagmar, adjusting her wide-brimmed black hat above her sunglasses. "Let me tell you how much I

1

loathe ... *despise* ... *detest* ... *abhor* and ... *abominate* human children."

"Oh, Dagmar, you're just mad because Cheyenne and Wally got away from us again," said Hedy.

This was not untrue. Cheyenne and Wally Shluffmuffin were the snotty ten-year-old orphans that Dagmar and Hedy had found in the Jolly Days Orphanage and chosen for a trial adoption. On their first night at Mandible House

2

in the hushed and lovely Dripping Fang Forest, Dagmar and Hedy got the twins settled in their cheery bedrooms and served them a nutritious all-chocolate welcome dinner. But after dinner the nosy kids began snooping about. And just because they discovered that Dagmar and Hedy were giant ants who were breeding a race of super-ants to replace mankind and end life on Earth as we know it, those ungrateful little brats ran away. Fortunately, Dagmar and Hedy were able to recapture them a scant few weeks later.

But on the cab ride back to Mandible House, the twins claimed to need a bathroom so badly they were about to poop their pants, and Dagmar had compassionately ordered the driver to stop at a gas station restroom. Cheyenne and Wally went in, locked the restroom doors, and escaped through the windows and into the cornfield before the Mandible sisters could catch them.

"Yes, I *am* mad that Cheyenne and Walter got away from us again," said Dagmar. "But that has little to do with how much I hate human children. Hate their soft spongy flesh. Hate their soft

3

horrid hair. Hate their watery little eyes. Hate their moist pink mouths. Hate the revolting heat that radiates from their limp, flabby bodies with the skeletons on the *inside* instead of on the *outside* where skeletons belong."

From beyond the white concrete restrooms adjoining the cornfield, the horn of a car began beeping loudly, angrily, and unceasingly. Dagmar pretended not to notice.

"So, dearest one, how do we get the repulsive little wretches back?" asked Hedy. "Run down the corn rows and hope to catch up with them?"

"No, no, nothing as tiresome as that," said Dagmar. "We need to get the big picture. We need to fly up above the cornfield and see where they're hiding."

"Unfortunately," said Hedy, "we're not the flying variety of ants."

"No," said Dagmar, "we're the *hiring* variety. Let's go to the nearest airport and hire ourselves a pair of wings."

The beeping of the horn was now so loud and so insistent, it was impossible to ignore. Taking their own sweet time about it, Dagmar and Hedy circled the restrooms and returned to the taxicab that was waiting for them, its meter running.

"All right, driver," Dagmar announced, approaching the cab, "there's been a slight change of plan. You will now drive us to the nearest airport that you know of where we can hire a pilot and a small crop-dusting plane."

"A pilot and a *what*?" shouted the driver, his face turning purple.

"I am certain you heard me," said Dagmar.

"First it's 'Drive us to Dripping Fang Forest,'" sputtered the driver. "Then it's 'No, drive us to a gas station.' Then it's 'No, drive us to a police station.' Then it's 'No, drive us to the FBI.' Then it's 'No, drive us to the Natural History Museum.' Now it's 'No, drive us to the nearest airport where we can hire a pilot and a small crop-dusting plane.' Well, I won't take any more of this, do you hear? I've *had* it with you people! I'm no longer driving you *anywhere*. Pay me the twenty-eight dollars and seventy-five cents that's on the meter right now and then get the heck out of my face!"

Dagmar walked right up to the door of the cab and leaned down so that her face was uncomfortably close to that of the driver.

"Please watch closely now," she said in a quiet voice.

She peeled away the bottom of her flesh-colored rubber human mask, revealing her horrible ant head with her gigantic black eyes, and her horrible mouth that looked like a huge pair of horrible black pliers, only sharper.

"Now then," she continued in a reasonable tone, "you have two choices. Choice A is to drive us to the nearest airport that you know of where we can hire a pilot and a small crop-dusting plane. Choice B is to have me pluck out your eyeballs and suck your brains from your skull through your eyeholes. Drive or pluck-and-suck—this is your choice. Which do you prefer?"

The cab driver seemed unable to speak. He made barely audible clicking noises in the back of his throat.

"Choice A or choice B," Dagmar repeated. "Choose one before I count to three, or I shall be forced to choose *for* you. Frankly, I prefer choice B, the pluck-and-suck. Ready? One . . . Two . . ."

"A!" croaked the cab driver, "choice A!"

"Choice A, *please, ma'am*," coached Dagmar, leaning closer.

"Choice A, *please, ma'am*," croaked the cab driver.

"What a pity," said Dagmar. "I was *so* in the mood for a little teatime snack of brains with eyeballs."

CHAPTER 2

Having a Vampire Dad Is Better Than Having a Zombie One

"I'm sure we've outrun them by now," said Cheyenne, huffing, puffing, sweating, gasping for breath, dabbing at her runny nose. "Don't you think we've outrun them by now?"

"I doubt it," Wally puffed.

Although Wally and Cheyenne Shluffmuffin were twins, their outlooks on life were quite different. Cheyenne saw only the good side of life, Wally only the bad. Cheyenne saw a puppy and thought frisky tricks and velvet ears. Wally saw a puppy and thought fleas, heartworm, and pooper-scoopers.

After at least half an hour of running down rows of cornstalks, Wally felt like his lungs were about to burst. Sweat was running down into his eyes.

"They could still be running after us," he said. "The Mandibles are way bigger than we are and way stronger. Did you know that ants can lift fifty times their own weight?"

"What does that have to do with whether we've outrun them?" Cheyenne asked. She sneezed hard enough to take off the top of her head.

"Nothing, really," said Wally. "I just thought you'd like to know."

"Well, thanks," said Cheyenne. "I appreciate it."

"You *appreciate* it?" said Wally. "Hey, if I didn't know you better, I'd swear that was sarcasm."

"It wasn't sarcasm," said Cheyenne, blowing her nose into a Kleenex. "I don't use sarcasm, Wally. Sarcasm is negative, and I'm a positive person. Unlike you, I choose to see the good in every person and in every situation."

"I know," said Wally, "and it drives me crazy. Tell me what's good about the situation we're in now, for instance."

"There are *lots* of things that are good about the situation we're in now."

"*Lots* means at least more than one," said Wally. "Name two things that are good about the situation we're in now."

"Okay," said Cheyenne. "One good thing is we escaped from Ont Dagmar and Ont Hedy."

"Please don't call them that, Cheyenne," said Wally. "They're *ants*, not *onts*. Ants that plan to . . . What's the second thing?"

"The second good thing is we're alive and healthy and we have our whole lives ahead of us," said Cheyenne. "We live in Cincinnati, the best darned city in the country, and we live in America, the best darned country in the world, and, and . . . You know, Wally, as long as you brought it up, I honestly don't see why you always have to be so negative."

"Really, Cheyenne? You don't see why I'm so

negative? How about the fact that we're *orphans*? How about the fact that Dad drowned in a Porta Potti and became a *zombie*?"

"Why are you calling Dad a zombie when you know Professor Spydelle *rejuvenated* him?"

"And turned him into a *vampire*! Why aren't you mentioning that?"

"Well, having a vampire dad is lots better than having a zombie one," said Cheyenne. "He isn't losing body parts all over the place now, and he doesn't smell so bad anymore. I just don't see why you always have to look at everything so negatively."

Wally wiped his face on his sleeve and looked around. The rows of corn seemed to go on forever. He had lost his sense of direction. He had absolutely no idea where they'd come from and where they should go. If they chose the wrong direction now, they were sure to run right into the arms of the Mandible sisters again.

"Cheyenne," said Wally, "look, I'm really sorry if I always sound negative to you. I really am, but you're so positive you just don't see the dangers that I do. I can't help it if . . ."

"*Ssshhh!*" Cheyenne held her finger up to her lips. "Do me a favor, Wally. Start over. Say whatever you were going to say, but try to say it in a positive way. Can you do that for me? Please?"

"Okay," said Wally. "Well, Cheyenne, you're my sister and I always try to protect you. I mean, you're my only living relative and I love you, okay? So I'd do anything to protect you. *Anything*. If your life was in danger, if somebody was trying to kill you, I'd attack them, even if they had guns and knives and I had just my bare hands. Even if they chopped my arms off and blood was spurting out of both of my stumps, I'd—"

"*Ssshhh,*" said Cheyenne, giving him a hug. "Why don't you just try to tell me what's good about the situation we're in right now?"

"Well," said Wally, "let me think. Okay. We're in a beautiful cornfield here, with lots of delicious fresh corn all around us that we could

eat ... and it's a warm sunny day ... and although I'm not exactly sure I remember what
direction we came from ... I guess that means
we can stay here as long as we like."

CHAPTER 3

Please Return Your Seat Backs to Their Upright and Locked Position in Preparation for Jumping Out of the Aircraft

Crop-dusting and sightseeing pilot Andy Barnes leaned back in his green vinyl La-Z-Boy lounge chair and put his feet up on his desk. With their sensitive antennae, the Mandible sisters could tell his sweat socks hadn't been washed in six days.

"Lemme get this straight," said Andy. Long blond hair hung over his eyes like a sheepdog's. He raked the hair back with his fingers and adjusted the curved visor of his faded red ball cap. "Y'all want me to take you up in a crop-dusting plane, but y'all don't want to dust crops?"

"That's right," said Dagmar. "We want to look for our poor little niece and nephew. They're only ten years old and they're lost in a cornfield not far from here. Poor things, they're probably frantic by now."

"What are they doing in a cornfield?"

"They crawled through a bathroom window in a gas station, dear," said Hedy.

"Why'd they do that?" Andy asked.

"Oh my." Hedy chuckled. "I'm afraid they were trying to get away from us. Isn't that silly?"

"It was just a game," Dagmar added quickly. "Hide-and-seek. But it got out of hand, as that game often does. The poor things just couldn't bear to be It."

"Being It made them . . . anxious," said Hedy. "Apprehensive, actually. And now, dear, we fear the worst."

"Why would you fear the worst?" said Andy.

"I mean, what could happen to them in a corn-field?"

"Well, corn could fall on them," said Dagmar. "From, you know, a rotten cornstalk. Or they could step in a gopher hole, snap off a foot, and bleed to death. Or someone could fly over the field in a small plane and strafe them with machine-gun fire. These things do happen. Can you take us up so we can look for them while they're still alive?"

"Sure thing, ma'am," said Andy. He jumped up from his desk, grabbed some gear, and hustled them out to the field.

The airfield was a tiny one. Two blacktopped runways split a wheat field, the blacktop cracked and potholed from the repeated freezing and melting snows of harsh Cincinnati winters. A row of small hangars stood decaying at the near end of the field.

Half a dozen single-engine planes crouched in readiness not far from the hangars, mostly Cess-nas and Piper Cubs, painted in perky colors. Andy guided them to a Skybolt biplane with three open cockpits in a row behind the propeller.

"We'll take the Skybolt," said Andy. "You gals ever flown before?"

The Mandible sisters shook their heads, deciding not to mention their brief but victorious fling at precision skydiving.

"Nothin' to it," said Andy. "First, put these on." He took two square canvas things with straps, slipped them over the sisters' shoulders, and buckled them in. "These here are your parachutes," he said. "No way you're ever gonna need these, but if you do, look down at the left side of your chest. See that flat steel ring with the piece of yellow tape on it?"

"Would that be what they call the rip cord?" asked Dagmar.

"Bingo," said Andy. "You pull 'er straight out from your body with both hands."

He guided Dagmar into the tiny cockpit directly behind the propeller and Hedy into the one just behind her. He fit each of them into a seat harness that went over the shoulders, around the thighs, chest, and waist, and buckled with a large aluminum quick-release lever.

"Do we pull the rip cord while we're still seated, dear?" asked Hedy.

Andy burst out laughing. "Oh no, *heck* no," he said. "If you need to jump, pull the quick-release lever on your seat harness, reach out for a wing strut, and pull yourself out of your seat. The wind will be buffeting you about pretty good, but place your feet carefully on both sides of the fuselage and then jump clear of the plane. Count to sixty, then pull the rip cord and float on down."

Andy handed each of them a leather helmet, a pair of goggles, and a pair of headphones with attached microphones.

"I'm gonna need to stow your hats and sunglasses now," he said, holding out his free hand.

The Mandible sisters looked alarmed.

"Why do we need to stow our hats and sunglasses?" asked Dagmar.

"If you don't, they'll blow off the second we get upstairs," said Andy. "The wind up there is somethin' fierce. You'll need to wear the helmets, the goggles, and the headsets just so we can talk."

Dagmar and Hedy exchanged looks, then handed him their hats and sunglasses.

Andy stared at Dagmar and Hedy and frowned.

"Pardon me for askin', ladies," he said, "but y'all aren't wearin' rubber *masks,* are you?"

"Yes, dear, we are," said Hedy.

"We were in a terrible fire many years ago and our faces are hideously disfigured," said Dagmar. "We were just trying to spare your feelings. I hope we don't disgust you."

"Oh, *heck* no, ma'am," said Andy uneasily. "I get *tons* of folks goin' for plane rides who were disfigured in fires, you'd be surprised." He stowed their hats and sunglasses behind a panel in the fuselage, then climbed quickly into the third cockpit.

As soon as Dagmar and Hedy put on their headgear, Andy started up the engine. He taxied to the landing strip, revved the motor loudly, then raced down the strip. Seconds later he pulled back on the joystick and the tiny plane leaped into the air. They were soon high over the airfield.

Far below them the hangars and planes looked like toys. The biplane seemed suspended in space, floating free. It was a marvelous feeling, the best feeling the Mandible sisters had had in years. For a moment they considered giving up breeding super-ants to replace mankind, and just devoting their lives to flying in small open-cockpit planes, but the moment didn't last.

It took less than five minutes to fly to the cornfield where the twins had disappeared.

"Circle the field," said Dagmar into her microphone.

"Roger that," said Andy. The small biplane hadn't completed more than half a circle before the Mandibles caught sight of something moving on the ground.

"Look!" shouted Dagmar. "Those two little specks off to the right there? I think it's the children!"

"I'll take 'er down for a closer look," said Andy into his headset.

The plane swooped low over the cornfield.

"It's them all right, poor darlings," said Hedy.

"Thank heavens they're still alive. Andy, can you land the plane?"

"Sure wish I could, ma'am," said Andy, "but I can't see a place big enough or flat enough to put 'er down."

"Are you telling us you refuse to land?" Dagmar asked.

"Ain't refusing," said Andy. "Just can't see a place to do it."

"Then can you take us up to fifteen hundred feet?" Dagmar asked.

"Why?"

"Because I asked you to and because I'm paying," said Dagmar. "Is that reason enough?"

"I reckon," said Andy. He pulled back on the joystick and the plane climbed steeply.

When the altimeter read fifteen hundred feet, which was high enough up for a person to jump and have the parachute open safely, Dagmar turned around and nodded to Hedy. They both yanked the quick-release levers on their seat harnesses. They grabbed a wing strut and pulled themselves out of their seats.

"Hey!" shouted Andy. "What the heck are you doing? Get back in your seats!"

The wind tugged at the Mandible sisters and almost tore them off the fuselage, but they held tightly to the struts.

"I said get back in your seats!" shouted Andy over the roar of the wind. "That's an order!"

"We don't take orders from humans!" yelled Dagmar.

She nodded to Hedy. Then they stepped off the fuselage into space.

CHAPTER 4

Terror in the Cornfield

As the sun sank lower in the late-afternoon sky, it threw long shadows down the rows of cornstalks. It had been griddle-hot in the field and quiet, except for the electric buzzing of the cicadas that rose in pitch with the temperature. Then the twins heard the sound of a small single-engine aircraft approaching.

Cheyenne and Wally became excited. They stood up and waved their arms, hoping the plane had spotted them. Two tiny figures fell out of the plane, then parachutes bloomed suddenly above them and the tiny figures floated earthward. Cheyenne and Wally watched them descend. There was something oddly familiar—

unpleasantly familiar—about these skydivers. And then Wally knew what it was.

"Cheyenne, it's *them*!" said Wally.

"What?" said Cheyenne. "Who?"

"*Them*. The Mandibles. The Onts."

"You're crazy, Wally. How *could* it be?"

"Trust me, it could! Run, Cheyenne! Run as fast as you can!"

Cheyenne and Wally took off down the row of cornstalks. Dagmar and Hedy, inspired by the nuptial flights of ant queens, had sharpened their skydiving skills on several Sundays at a jump site, and now expertly steered their chutes till they were only a few feet from the heads of the retreating children.

Dagmar threw herself onto Wally, Hedy threw herself onto Cheyenne, and both Onts wrestled the twins to the hard-packed earth.

"*Unh!*" cried Wally, as the breath was knocked out of him.

"*Oof!*" cried Cheyenne, her fall broken by cornstalks.

Wally punched Dagmar in the stomach as

hard as he could and gasped in pain. Instead of encountering soft and yielding flesh, his knuckles had hit Dagmar's bony exoskeleton. The pain throbbed in his hand. He hit her again and again. She grabbed his hands and imprisoned them in her viselike claws. Hedy pinned Cheyenne to the ground. The children were no match for giant ants who could carry fifty times their own weight.

"Stupid insect!" Wally blurted.

"Stupid human!" Dagmar hissed.

The Mandible sisters dragged the still-struggling Shluffmuffin twins back down the corn row to the end of the field by their wrists, then around the white concrete-block buildings to the gas station.

There was only one car at the self-service pumps, an old Ford station wagon. The hood was raised and a hose ran from the pump to the Ford's gas tank. A weary-looking woman with white hair, and dressed in a blue denim jumpsuit, was checking her oil as Mandibles dragged the Shluffmuffins around the corner.

"Help!" yelled Wally. "My sister and I are being kidnapped!"

"Their names are Dagmar and Hedy Mandible, and they're kidnapping us!" yelled Cheyenne. "Call the police!"

The woman in the blue denim jumpsuit looked alarmed.

"We're also orphans," added Wally, "in case that makes us more sympathetic."

"Don't pay any attention to them, dear," said Hedy to the weary-looking woman. "These are very bad children. We're taking them home to be disciplined." She turned to Cheyenne. "No more cable TV for the rest of the week for *you*, young lady!"

"These creatures are lying!" said Wally. "They may look like women, but they're not, they're giant ants! They're breeding a race of super-ants in the basement to—"

"—replace mankind and end life on Earth as we know it! Is that a riot or what?" said Dagmar to the woman. Then Dagmar turned back to Wally. "Why don't you get a more believable

29

story, Walter? Why don't you say we discipline you because you and your sister snatch old ladies' purses and swipe things from toy stores?"

The woman looked somewhat relieved. "Kids these days," she said, shaking her head. "I don't know."

"You've got to believe us!" cried Cheyenne. "They really are giant ants!"

Dagmar dragged Wally up to the raised hood of the station wagon.

"How's this car of yours run, dear?" Dagmar asked the woman. "Any serious mechanical problems?"

"Not really," said the woman with a smile. "It does burn a little oil, but I can't complain, not after a hundred and twenty thousand miles."

"Good," said Dagmar. "Then it'll do."

"Excuse me?" said the woman.

"We're going to need your station wagon now, Grandma," said Dagmar. "Drop the hood and step aside."

"I beg your *pardon*?" said the woman. The alarmed look was back on her face.

"It turns out we're lying and the kids were telling the truth," said Dagmar. "How ironic is *that*?"

"We really *are* giant ants, dear," said Hedy. "And we really *are* planning to replace mankind and end life on Earth as we know it. So you'd better do as we say. We're quite nasty."

The woman's eyes bugged out like a toad's. Her mouth opened wide enough to catch fruit bats.

"Step aside, Granny, or I'll bite your arm off," said Dagmar. She raised the edge of her rubber mask and let the woman gaze at her horrible insect face.

The woman began backing slowly away from her car, as if sleepwalking.

Dagmar slammed down the hood of the station wagon with a loud *whump*. She opened a back door, grabbed Wally by the collar of his shirt and the waist of his jeans, and threw him inside like a sack of sweet potatoes. Then she threw Cheyenne in after him.

As Hedy stood by without helping, Dagmar

yanked the hose out of the gas tank and hurled it to the ground. It writhed there like a wounded bull snake, bleeding gasoline. Then she climbed into the backseat and rolled down the window.

"Would you like to drive us home now, Hedy darling?" said Dagmar in a voice dripping with sarcasm. "Or would you rather wait till that woman snaps out of her stupor and phones the Ohio State Troopers?"

CHAPTER 5

A Crash Course in
Salesmanship

"I have called this meeting," said Hortense Jolly, "to discuss the current adoption program here at the Jolly Days Orphanage of Cincinnati."

Thirty-six orphans with smudged faces and threadbare clothes, ranging in age from six to thirteen, sat cross-legged on the floor, gazing up at the owner of their orphanage.

"As you know," said Hortense Jolly, "despite the recent placement of Cheyenne and Wally Shluffmuffin, who have had, I'll admit, a, uh, minor setback with their new adoptive parents, our adoption rate here has been somewhat disappointing. We haven't had a single other adoption for, let me see now . . . sixteen months. Although it's hard to point to any one factor that might have caused this situation, frankly, children, I blame *you*."

The thirty-six orphans didn't ask why they were being blamed for not having been adopted. They were used to being blamed.

"You know every time one of you is adopted I get a six-hundred-dollar adoption fee," said Hortense. "You know I generously kick back a shiny new penny to each of you every time that happens. So why aren't you helping me get you adopted?"

"How could we help you do that?" asked a little girl named Ellie Mae.

"How?" said Hortense. "I'll tell you how. By realizing you're a product and by asking yourself, How can I sell this product to prospective adopters? Every grown-up you meet is a prospective adopter. You must convince these people you're the kid they didn't know they wanted. You must put yourself in their shoes. You must ask yourself: How would *their* lives be better if they adopted you? How would adopting you fulfill a need of *theirs*? Case in point: The Mandible sisters came here looking for orphans who had horrible allergies and stinky feet. Cheyenne's nose never stops leaking, and Wally's feet stink worse than barn animals. I put them together with the Mandible sisters and—presto!— I made a sale. That, kids, is the secret of making a sale: One, we meet a prospect. Two, we identify a need of theirs that we can fill. And three, we make them think that we have filled it."

"What's a prospect?" asked Rocco, the bully.

"A prospect is any grown-up who you meet," said Hortense. "Who can name some grown-ups that we meet here at Jolly Days during the day?"

"The postman!" screamed a girl named Penny.

"Good, Penny," said Hortense. "Yes, everyone you meet is a prospect, even the postman. So, next time you see the postman, why not say, 'Boy, Mr. Postman, that mailbag sure looks heavy. You know, if I was your kid, I could carry it for you. Have you ever thought of becoming a

parent?' Who can name another grown-up that we meet here at Jolly Days during the day?"

"The exterminator!" shrieked a boy named Orville.

"Good, Orville," said Hortense. "So, next time you see the exterminator, why not say, 'Gosh, Ms. Exterminator, that rat poison sure looks dangerous. If I was your kid, I could spread it around for you. Have you ever thought of becoming a mom?'"

"What if she has kids already?" asked a boy named Otto.

"Better yet," said Hortense, "because then you can skip the step of convincing her to *become* a parent. Tell her two kids don't take up much more space than one—just throw another mattress on the floor like we do *here*."

"What do we do if she doesn't want any more kids?" asked a girl named Sue-Ann.

"Then we make her feel *guilty,* Sue-Ann. We tell her how you long for a mommy or a daddy. We tell her you're so miserable without a mommy or daddy, you cry yourself to sleep every night. You remember that nice Professor Spydelle who came here and looked you over?"

"The British guy?" said a big boy named Wayne. "He smoked a pipe? I swiped his watch."

"That's the one," said Hortense. "He told us he was interested in adopting one of you— maybe even more than one of you. Remember that?"

"Yeah," said Wayne. "But he was a stinking liar. He never came back."

"Right," said Hortense. "But a couple of days ago I called his wife. You know what happened when I told her how disappointed you were that they didn't adopt you? That you were so disappointed it made you cry softly in the corner?"

"What?" said Wayne.

"She cried," said Hortense. "Which tells me she's still a *very* hot prospect. So, kids, I thought up a plan: We're going to rent a bus, and we're all going to visit the Spydelles in their home in Dripping Fang Forest. We're going to put on a little show for them, with songs and every-thing—just like a Broadway musical. I've al-ready written some of the songs. We're going to make the Spydelles feel so guilty, they can't refuse to adopt at least one or two of you—maybe even more. Oh yes, there is one tiny problem. It turns out Mrs. Spydelle is a giant spider. Any of you have a problem with a mom who's a giant spider?"

"*Eeeuuww!* That's gross!" said a girl named Emmy-Lou. "Does she bite?"

"I've been assured that she doesn't bite," said Hortense.

"How come Professor Spydelle married a *spider*?" asked a boy named Elijah.

"That I didn't quite understand," said Hor-tense. "But people do *lots* of things I don't understand."

"Did he know she was a spider when he married her?" asked Elijah.

"We didn't discuss that," said Hortense. "But the Spydelles told me they have a wonderful big house in the woods and they *love* children. Any of you willing to have a mom who's a giant spider in order to get a wonderful big house in the woods with real parents who love children? Let me see hands."

A little girl named Rosie tentatively raised her hand.

"Okay, good, there's one. Thank you, Rosie," said Hortense. "Anybody else? Come on, people, work with me here."

A couple more orphans raised their hands.

"Tell you what," said Hortense. "Every orphan who gets adopted by the giant spider gets not *one* shiny new penny but *ten*. No, wait a minute, I'm going to do even better than that—any orphan who gets adopted by the giant spider gets *fifty* shiny new pennies!"

Several more hands went up.

"*Now* we're rolling," said Hortense, rubbing her hands together. "*Now* we're cooking. *Now* we're getting somewhere. All right, kids, we're going to put on an entertaining and informative show for the Spydelles—think of it as a musical infomercial. First rehearsal starts in the dining hall in an hour. I'm going to teach you your first song. I'm calling it 'Could We Love a Spider Mommy?' Rocco, bring your ukulele! Rosie, bring your bongo drums! Otto, bring your tuba!"

CHAPTER 6

If You Must Carjack, Please Be Polite

As the sun began to set, the old Ford station wagon sped out of the city along the interstate. Wally sat in the back between Dagmar and Cheyenne. He noticed that the lady who owned the car had attached several small framed photographs of smiling children to the sun visors and the dashboard. Wally felt awful that she had lost her car, but worse that she'd lost her photographs. The smiling children were probably her grandchildren. He missed his own tiny grandma Gloria.

"I think the way you treated that old lady sucked," said Wally.

Cheyenne caught Wally's eye and shook her head.

"Who cares what *you* think?" said Dagmar.

"It was bad enough you took her car," said Wally. "Why did you have to insult her, too?"

Cheyenne kicked Wally in the ankle, hoping that would shut him up.

"Taking her car was something I *had* to do," said Dagmar. "Insulting her was just for fun."

"You're disgusting," said Wally. "You make me want to puke."

Cheyenne sighed and closed her eyes.

"If you're trying to ingratiate yourself with your captors, dear," said Hedy, "it's not working."

Hedy drove awhile in silence. Wally was desperately trying to come up with a plan for saving them. Cheyenne was desperately trying to find some good in their situation. She blew her nose into another tissue. Hedy snatched it out of Cheyenne's hands and stuffed it in her purse.

"Since you're going to kill us anyway," said Wally, "I might as well tell you: It was *me* who thought up the plan to say we had to go to the john and then escape through the restroom window. Cheyenne had nothing to do with it."

"That is *so* not true," said Cheyenne, kicking him again. "It was *me* who thought that one up *entirely.*"

"Cheyenne, you lie like a rug," said Wally. "She's just trying to take credit for my ideas because she can't think up any of her own."

Cheyenne kicked him again.

"That was very noble of you both, my darlings," said Hedy, "each of you trying to sacrifice yourself for the other. But it was rather a bit too obvious, don't you think?"

They drove on in silence.

Our only chance, thought Wally, *will come on the walk from the car to the house. If we can't find a way to break away from them on the walk between the car and the house, then we are really, really, really dead meat.*

CHAPTER 7

Why, Doctor,
What Big Teeth You Have

In his volunteer's starched white lab coat with the distinctive American Red Cross insignia on the shoulder, Vampire Dad escorted the next blood donor into his cubicle in the bloodmobile and had her lie down on a cot. He tied a short piece of rubber tubing around her arm till a vein bulged out. Next he took a piece of sterile cotton, moistened it with rubbing alcohol, and briskly swabbed the vein. Then he took a sterile needle, which was attached to a plastic tube, and stuck it into her vein.

"Ouch!" said the woman. "That hurt."

"Sorry," said Dad. He had missed the vein entirely. He tried again.

"Ouch!" said the woman. "You're stabbing me!"

"Sorry," said Dad. "Sometimes those little veiny buggers really try to get away from you." He stuck the needle into her arm again.

"*Ouch!*" said the woman. "Hey, have you ever done this before?"

"Thousands of times, madam," said Dad. And that time he nailed it.

Now came the part he liked best, the tube slowly filling with exquisite crimson liquid. Blood like the most succulent grape juice. Blood like the most exquisite burgundy wine. He inhaled its bouquet through the plastic, and the fumes made him dizzy with anticipation. It was all he could do to keep from licking the tube as he removed it, put a cap on it, and inserted another empty tube into the one attached to the needle. It was all he could do not to dispense with the needle and the tubes altogether, and just bury his fangs in the soft pale flesh of the donors and suck their veins till they were as flat, thin, and dry as uncooked angel hair pasta.

A white-coated woman named Miss Prentiss stuck her head in the door of the cubicle.

"Dr. Shluffmuffin, may I see you a moment?"

"Uh, sure, Miss Prentiss," said Dad. "Right now, you mean?"

"Yes, please, right now."

Miss Prentiss was the director of the blood-mobile. The princess of plasma. The high priestess of hemoglobin. The reason she'd called him *Doctor* Shluffmuffin was that he'd fibbed and told her he was a doctor when he applied for the job. He'd thought he would have a better chance of getting hired that way.

Not telling her he was a vampire was another fib, but explaining *why* he was seemed too complicated—that he'd drowned in a freak Porta Potti accident and come back to life as a zombie, that a friend of his kids had cured the zombiism but turned him into a vampire.

"Dr. Shluffmuffin, there have been a number of complaints," said Miss Prentiss.

"Not about *me*, I hope," said Vampire Dad.

"I'm afraid so," said Miss Prentiss. "By the

way, you *are* a doctor, aren't you? At Cincinnati General, I believe you said?"

"Yes, yes, of course. Cincinnati General. Blood department. Why?"

"Because some of the donors have complained that you didn't seem to know how to put a needle into their arms."

"Oh, ha-ha, did you hear about that?" said Dad. "I just had a teensy bit of trouble finding a vein on one of the first donors. That happens sometimes."

"Nineteen donors complained you had trouble finding a vein."

"Well, I certainly don't think it was *nineteen*," said Dad. "It was one or two donors. Is that what this is about, my having trouble finding veins on three or four donors?"

"No, it's something else."

"I see. Well then, what's the problem?"

"It's hard to be specific, Dr. Shluffmuffin," said Miss Prentiss. "It's not a complaint exactly, it's more a general feeling that we've been getting. A feeling that you're, um . . . Let me put it

50

another way. We at the American Red Cross do like our volunteers to be enthusiastic about their work, but *your* level of enthusiasm is well . . . up-setting. I'm afraid we're going to have to ask you to turn in your white coat and your syringe. You're just making the staff too nervous."

"I do not believe this," said Dad. "You're *firing* me? From a volunteer's job I am doing for *free*?"

"I'm sorry, Dr. Shluffmuffin. This is harder for me than it is for you."

"I doubt that," said Dad. "You know, this comes at a really bad time for me personally. I mean, I'm having family troubles at home, *big* time."

"I didn't realize," said Miss Prentiss. "Dr. Shluffmuffin, I'm sorry you're having troubles at home, but it doesn't really affect our decision. I'm afraid that we simply—"

"My own children have *disowned* me," said Dad, "so do you think you could possibly cut me some slack? They've chosen to let them-selves be adopted by some British professor and an enormous . . ."

"An enormous . . . ?"

". . . spider," Dad mumbled, sensing he might be revealing a wee bit too much.

"I'm sorry, doctor," said Miss Prentiss, "the word you just said was *spider*?"

"Yes, *spider,*" said Dad, deciding the unfairness of his situation would seem worse than its weirdness and win him an ally. "My children would rather live with an enormous *spider* than with their own *father.*"

"Uh-huh. Yes. *Hmm.* My, my. Well. You know, it's been interesting chatting with you, Dr. Shluffmuffin, but I really must get back to work now, so if you don't mind . . ."

"Okay, okay, okay, I'll go then," said Dad. "I certainly wouldn't want to stay at a job where I'm not appreciated."

"Good," said Miss Prentiss.

"Do you think I could at least take a small souvenir of my experience here?" Dad asked. "It would mean a lot to me."

"What sort of . . . souvenir did you have in mind?"

"Oh, you know, anything at all," said Dad. "A length of the rubber tubing that we use to tie around a donor's arm ... a syringe ... a bag of blood ... anything."

"All right, Dr. Shluffmuffin, unless you leave here immediately, I'm afraid I'm going to have to ..." She stuck her head out the door and shouted, "Security? May I have some help in here now? *Armed* help?"

"I'm *going,* I'm *going,*" said Dad.

CHAPTER 8

You Can't Go Home Again—
Seriously, You Can't

At last the old Ford station wagon slowed down, and Hedy clicked on her left turn signal. The car pulled off the interstate and entered the dense woods beneath a tall archway surrounded by nearly tropical vegetation. A big sign read: DRIPPING FANG FOREST.

Next to the sign that read: DRIPPING FANG FOREST was a smaller sign. It read: PRIVATE PROPERTY. KEEP OUT. THIS MEANS YOU. TRESPASSERS WILL BE... The word PROSECUTED had been crossed out, and somebody had written SHOT above it. The word SHOT had been crossed out, and somebody had written TORN APART BY WOLVES above that. The words TORN APART BY WOLVES had been crossed out, and above that somebody had carefully printed RIPPED OPEN AND WILL HAVE THEIR GLISTENING RED GUTS STRUNG BETWEEN THE TREES LIKE WET LAUNDRY.

The unpaved road into the woods progressed from tooth-sized pebbles to gravel the consistency of kitty litter to the matted grass of crop circles. When the overhead vines grasping at the car made further forward movement impossible, Hedy turned off the motor.

"Everybody out, my darlings," said Hedy. She got out of the driver's seat and came around to the back, opened the door, and led Cheyenne out of the car, her black-gloved hand gripping the girl's slim wrist.

Dagmar clamped her gloved hand onto Wally's thicker wrist tightly enough to restrict blood flow and yanked him out of the back of the car. In the gathering darkness, Mandibles pulled Shluffmuffins along the path through the woods like nannies leading feisty three-year-olds.

"In case you people are plotting another cute getaway," said Dagmar, "make my day. Give me an excuse to snap off three or four of your fingers."

We've got to do something and we've got to do it fast, thought Wally. *Because as hard as it might be to get away from them now, it will be a whole lot harder once we get inside Mandible House and they lock us in our bedrooms with their colorful quilts and puffy pillows.*

A cloud of tiny gnats suddenly hovered about Wally's head. They blundered into his eyes, ears, mouth, and nostrils. Wally coughed and spat and tried to wave them away. Thorny branches and bushes with burrs caught at Cheyenne's clothing, making small rips in the cloth and scratching her skin till it was spiderwebbed with delicate threads of blood.

Looking on the bright side, thought Cheyenne, *this could have been worse. We could have been adopted by cannibals, piranhas, or giant flesh-eating streptococcus bacteria instead of giant ants.*

And then up ahead, looming like a monster in the forest's gloom, was Mandible House.

This is it, thought Wally. *It's now or never.* He leaned close to Cheyenne's ear.

"When they unlock the door, we're splitting," he whispered. "Just do what *I* do."

"What did you just whisper to your sister, Walter?" Dagmar demanded.

"I just told her how bee-*yoo*-tee-full you are," said Wally.

Dagmar slapped at him, but Wally ducked.

As Hedy was unlocking the big front door, Wally nodded to Cheyenne. They took a deep breath, then shoved their captors off balance and twisted their wrists free of ant-claw grips. Hedy grabbed Cheyenne by the hair. Cheyenne screamed. Wally hurled himself clear of Dagmar and raced into the woods.

"Walter, you get back in this house immediately!" Dagmar demanded.

"Oh, right," called Wally, "like *that's* going to happen."

"You will pay dearly for this, I promise you!" shouted Dagmar. "You will rue the day you disobeyed me, mark my words!"

"Tell you what, Dagmar," Wally called, "let's make a deal: You let my sister go and I'll surrender!"

"No!" yelled Cheyenne. "Don't listen to him, Dagmar!"

"I'm serious," called Wally. "Free Cheyenne and you can have me!"

"Don't listen to him!" yelled Cheyenne. "I'll be fine, Wally! I always am! Save *yourself*!"

"Thanks for the offer, Walter," said Dagmar, "but it's not acceptable! We must have you both!"

"No way!" yelled Wally. "Cheyenne, I'll get you out of there soon, I promise!"

"I wouldn't hold my breath if I were you, Cheyenne dear," said Hedy.

"If you don't give yourself up, Walter, we will starve your sister to death!" Dagmar shouted. "Do you hear me? We will not feed Cheyenne a single forkful of food until you surrender! Think it over!"

And then the big door clanged shut. Wally felt sick to his stomach at having to abandon his twin sister to the giant ants, but he told himself that he had a lot better shot at saving her from the outside.

CHAPTER 9

Warning: It Is a Violation of a Cincinnati City Ordinance to Lick Your Fellow Passenger

Fresh from the humiliation of being fired from the Red Cross bloodmobile, Vampire Dad boarded a city bus. He had to regain his composure before returning to Dripping Fang Forest and the Spydelles and the indignity of sleeping in their garage.

How could Cheyenne and Wally have dumped him for the Spydelles? How could his own dear children prefer a disgusting giant spider and a pipe-smoking professor with a phony British accent to a loving father, vampire or no? How had they forgotten the years he'd spent with them before his death, changing their diapers, nursing them when they were sick, comforting them when they were frightened, soothing them when they were upset, teaching them to walk and talk and wipe their butts and tie their shoes and ride a bike and develop self-confidence and treat others with dignity? How did all of that get thrown out the window just because, through no fault of his own, he'd developed a teensy thirst for human blood?

He had to get them back. He had to. He *would* get them back. Whatever the Spydelles had done to steal their love, he would do more and make them love him better. He needed to earn money to buy things for Cheyenne and Wally. Books. Computers. New clothes. He had to find a safer way to earn money. Before his death he'd been an orthodontist. Maybe he could do that again. Sure, why not! There were lots of people walking around Cincinnati with weird-looking teeth. Speaking of which, maybe he'd grind down his own fangs a little, make himself a retainer to wear while he slept.

He had learned so much about life before his tragic drowning. He could teach the twins so many things that would help them become happy and successful adults. He could teach them that all bullies are cowards—if you stand up to them, they'll back off. He could teach them that if you spit on a pencil eraser you can erase ink. He could teach Wally to be a little less pessimistic. He could teach Cheyenne to be a little *more* pessimistic. He would show them who their *real* father was, and he wouldn't let this stupid, insane, compulsive, overwhelming, all-encompassing craving for blood get in his way. It was a weakness—just like the weakness others had for alcohol or gambling or chocolate—and he would overcome it!

The bus hadn't gone more than three blocks through the darkening city when Dad became aware that the woman in the seat beside him was having a problem. She began sniffing and snorting, and then she muttered, "Oh no, not again." She held her nose, leaned her head way back, and stared straight up.

"Are you all right, miss?" Dad asked.

"I'll be okay," said the woman. "It's no big deal."

"What seems to be the problem?" Dad asked.

"Just a stupid nosebleed," said the woman.

"Ah," said Dad. He peered closely at her. She was pinching her nose with the thumb and first finger of her right hand. A thin trickle of red began dripping down her wrist and into the sleeve of her blouse.

"Is there anything I can do to help?" Dad asked.

"No, no thanks," said the woman. "Sorry if this is grossing you out."

"Not at all," said Dad, "not at all."

If I can just remain calm, he thought, *I'll be all right. If I can just control myself and not cause a scene in a public place. If I can just restrain myself from leaning over and licking that trickle of blood as it runs down her wrist and into her sleeve, everything will be fine.*

He watched the trickle intently.

What a waste, he thought. *Blood that nobody needs, blood that isn't any good to anybody, blood that can never be used for transfusions or any other useful purpose is dripping down this woman's wrist, staining her blouse, lost forever. What a waste! What a tragic waste to see human blood running undrunk when thirsty vampires in undeveloped countries can't get the nourishment they so desperately need!*

The woman continued to snuffle and drip. Dad couldn't take his eyes off her. He tried hard to restrain himself from leaning over and licking her nose. He tried so hard he shook. But then, he could control himself no longer. With a sigh of resignation, he leaned over and slurped the red trickle with his long red tongue.

"What are you *doing*?" the woman shrieked.

"Sorry," Dad mumbled.

He jumped up, yanked the overhead emergency cord, and leaped off the bus.

CHAPTER 10

Get to Know Your Jailer

Dagmar took Cheyenne upstairs and guided her into her old bedroom.

"Well, here we are," said Dagmar. "Just as you left it. I have to go now, but feel free to watch an educational program on TV. Or play mindless video games to rot your brain."

Cheyenne hadn't eaten in hours and was pretty hungry.

"When's dinner?" she asked.

"Twenty minutes past never," said Dagmar. She left and locked the door behind her.

So what Dagmar shouted at Wally wasn't an empty threat, Cheyenne thought. *All right, I'll just have to get used to not eating, that's all. Fasting is sup-*

posed to really clear your mind and focus your thinking. Some of the world's greatest thinkers were famous for fasting. Like that guy in India, Gandhi, and, uh . . . She couldn't think of anyone else but Gandhi just then. *I wonder how long you can go without eating. Probably not that long. How awful that I might die with Dad thinking Wally and I don't love him. I have to tell him the truth, but how can I do that if I'm stuck here, starving to death? If only I can find a way to escape. If only we could go back in time to the day Dad drowned and keep him from entering that Porta Potti. Who do we know that might be able to teach us about time travel? The professor?*

Somebody was unlocking the door. It swung open and Hedy entered. She removed her wide-brimmed black hat and sunglasses and placed them on the desk.

"You must be exhausted, dear," said Hedy, "after your ordeal in the cornfield."

"Not really," said Cheyenne. She sneezed and blew her nose into a tissue.

"*Gesundheit,* dear," said Hedy, snatching the tissue out of her hands. "Why don't you lie

67

down on your bed, with its gaily colored quilt and its puffy pillows, and listen as I tell you a bit about ant culture."

"Whatever," said Cheyenne. She lay down on the bed.

"You may keep your eyes open or closed," said Hedy, "but I want you to listen to the sound of my voice. And I want you to imagine that as I speak your body is filling up with lovely warm liquid. Lovely warm liquid spreading from the tips of your toes right up to the top of your head."

Lovely warm liquid spreading from the tips of my toes to the top of my head? thought Cheyenne. *What's she trying to do, hypnotize me? It won't work. You can't hypnotize somebody if they don't want you to.*

"You may feel drowsy or you may not, dear," said Hedy, "but are you imagining the lovely warm liquid filling up your body from your toes to your head?"

"Uh-huh," said Cheyenne. *I won't let her hypnotize me, but that lovely warm liquid filling up my body wouldn't be so bad if it was soup. Like steaming minestrone with garden vegetables, tender cuts of lean beef, savory herbs and spices . . .*

Cheyenne's stomach growled. She stifled a yawn.

"It's perfectly all right to yawn," said Hedy. "It means you're beginning to relax. Has the lovely warm liquid reached your waist, dear?"

"Uh-huh," said Cheyenne. *Or seasoned meatballs, vibrant spinach, and tender pearl-shaped pasta in a rich chicken broth. Mmm . . .*

"Good," said Hedy. "Well, to begin with, ants have been around for a hundred million years. They live in very large colonies, and every colony is ruled by a queen. The queen is fifty to a hundred times as big as the other ants. She spends her whole life laying eggs. Thousands of eggs. Millions of eggs. The workers are females, too, and they do all the work. The larger females are the soldiers, and they defend the colony. At certain times of the year, many types of ants produce winged males and queens. They fly into the air and mate. Then the males die and each queen establishes a new nest. Has the lovely warm liquid reached your chest, dear?"

"Uh-huh." *Or thick and creamy New England clam chowder with parsley, celery, onions, and hearty pieces of clam. Mmm ...*

"Good," said Hedy. "Let's continue. Ants grow fungus on leaves and use it as food. And some kinds of ants keep aphids the way humans keep cows—they milk them. The aphids produce a sweet milky juice. The ant's abdomen contains two stomachs. One holds food that it uses itself and the second stomach stores food that it shares with the rest of the colony. Has the lovely warm liquid reached your neck, dear?"

"Uh-huh," said Cheyenne. *Feeling woozy ... Must fight to stay awake ... Must not let myself get hypnotized ... Must not ...*

"Do you know about the slave-making ants?" said Hedy. "They have nifty ways to make slaves out of other kinds of ants. In Africa the queen of the *Bothriomyrmex decapitans* ants lets herself be dragged by the *Tapinoma* ants into their nest. As soon as she's in the nest, she bites

70

off the head of the *Tapinoma* queen and starts laying her own eggs. She enslaves the *Tapinoma* worker ants, and they take care of her eggs."

Hedy looked at Cheyenne carefully.

"Has the lovely warm liquid reached the top of your head yet, dear?"

"Uh-huh," said Cheyenne dreamily.

"I'm going to pinch your arm now," said Hedy, "but you won't feel a thing."

"Uh-huh," said Cheyenne.

Hedy reached over and gave Cheyenne's arm a hard pinch.

"Did you feel that, dear?" Hedy asked.

"Feel what?" said Cheyenne.

"Feel what, *Ont Hedy*," said Hedy.

"Feel what, *Ont Hedy*," said Cheyenne.

"Would you like to meet the babies, dear?" Hedy asked.

"Uh-huh," said Cheyenne.

Hedy helped Cheyenne stand up. The girl swayed unsteadily on her feet. Hedy took her by the arm and slowly led her down to the cellar to meet the super-larvae.

Cheyenne gazed at the hundreds of slimy, eyeless, Chihuahua-sized worms in their cardboard containers. She felt strangely calm and peaceful. She felt full of lovely warm chunky split pea and ham soup with natural hickory-smoked flavor. She no longer felt hungry.

Ch-ch-ch-ch-ch . . . , chattered the larvae. *Ch-ch-ch-ch-ch . . .*

Hedy steered Cheyenne over to the Snot Press and the odor-extracting machine.

"Let me show you how we feed the babies," said Hedy gently, placing the girl's hands on the stainless steel crank of the Snot Press.

While dripping the thick grayish-green liquid into the piranha-like little mouths, Cheyenne got too close to the larvae and one of them fastened itself onto her thumb. The suction of the larva's mouth was surprisingly strong. Hedy immediately yanked Cheyenne's hand clear.

There were teeth marks in a little ring around Cheyenne's thumb, each of them marked by a tiny freckle of blood, like sprinkles on frozen yogurt. Cheyenne felt nothing.

"Come with me, dear," said Hedy.

"Uh-huh," said Cheyenne.

Hedy took Cheyenne to the bathroom, doused her thumb with hydrogen peroxide, and wrapped it in a Winnie the Pooh Band-Aid. Then she led Cheyenne back to her bedroom.

"Good night, dear," said Hedy. "I'm locking you in for the night for your own safety and comfort."

"Uh-huh," said Cheyenne.

When Hedy left, Cheyenne noticed the wide black hat and sunglasses that Hedy had left behind. She dreamily tried them on and posed in front of the full-length mirror.

Hedy walked into Dagmar's bedroom and sat down on the bed.

"So how did your little hypnotherapy session go?" Dagmar asked.

"She was a perfect subject," said Hedy. "I was able to implant a couple of key phrases in her subconscious. You know, dear, the girl seems very cooperative. I think she just might be more useful to us alive than dead."

"Why on earth would you think that?" Dagmar asked. *Hmmm. Where did this sympathy for a human come from? Has Hedy's unsettling sympathy toward humans been extended to others? At what point does sympathy toward humans edge into disloyalty toward onts?*

"Well, I mean, what good would she be to us dead?" asked Hedy.

"What do you *mean* what good would she be to us dead?" said Dagmar. "Tell the class, Hedy: How do we process human children?"

Hedy sighed.

"Come on, Hedy," said Dagmar. "What's the recipe for human-child-burger-on-a-sesame-seed-bun?"

Hedy made a sour face, then repeated the familiar ont nursery rhyme in a singsong voice:

We let the body ripen for a week.
The meat is soft and has a pleasant reek.
We grind it up and shape it into patties.
We pop it on the grill for moms and daddies.

"Or babies," said Dagmar. "Don't forget the babies *love* human-child-burgers. Although they do tend to prefer it raw."

"Right," said Hedy. "You know, dear, if we do kill Cheyenne, we'll be losing a wonderful source of snot. More importantly, though, we'll be losing an ally in our great plan of replacing mankind and ending life on Earth as we know it."

"Do you really think your hypnosis can get this human girl to betray her entire race to help *onts*?"

"There is absolutely no doubt in my mind whatever, dear," said Hedy.

CHAPTER 11

A Guilty Secret Revealed

When Edgar Spydelle came into his and Shirley's bedroom, he found his wife sitting in the middle of their web hammock, spinning silk from her spinnerets.

"Oh, there you are, Edgar dear," said Shirley. "I was just making you another pair of pajamas."

"You don't have to do that, darling," said Edgar. "I already have eleven."

"The well-dressed professor can't have too many pajamas," said Shirley, continuing to spin. "You seem a bit pensive, Edgar. Is everything all right?"

"No, I'm afraid not, actually."

"Why, what is it, Edgar? Has something I've done displeased you?"

"No, no, of course not. It's something that's been troubling me. Something I haven't told you about Cheyenne and Wally, and it's making me feel dreadful."

"What is it?"

"Well," said Edgar, "you know the twins have enormous affection for us both..."

"Yes...?"

"But when they told their father that they loved us more than him and wanted us to adopt them... Well, I suspect they were fibbing. They knew how much you wanted children, and they knew what would happen if we had our own. They were trying to save my life, and I'm afraid I let them."

Shirley sagged like an inflated parade-balloon that had just sprung a leak.

"Oh, Edgar," said Shirley. "Poor Mr. Shluff-muffin. How awful he must feel."

"I know," said Edgar.

"We have to tell him," said Shirley.

"Tell him what?"

"Why, the truth, of course."

"B-b-but if we did that, my love . . ."

"Yes?"

"Well, I mean, then we'd have to give the twins back . . ."

"Yes . . ."

"And you'd feel so bereft, you'd probably insist on having some children of our own . . ."

"I suppose so . . ."

"And after mating, dear, you, being a spider, would, needless to say, need to, you know, devour me . . ."

Shirley sighed.

"Oh, Edgar," she said, "do try not to take that personally."

CHAPTER 12

Can You Sneak Back into Prison?

*F*or the past hour Wally had been circling Mandible House, trying to come up with a plan to rescue Cheyenne. He didn't dare think about what the Onts might be doing to her; he just knew he had to somehow get his sister out of there.

He could try to sneak back inside the house. Use his trusty Swiss Army knife to unscrew the screws that held the stainless steel bars in place over the windows, creep back in, and lie low till the Onts went to bed, then sneak Cheyenne out as he'd done the first time.

Was it too risky? Was there too great a chance that he'd be caught and locked up again and lose the advantage he had in being free? Of course. But never mind that. This plan appealed to the commando in him.

The wind sighed through the pine trees. Wally carefully and quietly began climbing the vines that hung down the sides of the building to get to an upstairs window. Four feet from his goal, he lost his footing. He slipped and nearly fell to his death on the ground below, but at the last moment was able to grab on to some vines to slow his fall. His hands were raw from being used as brake pads, the vines whizzing through them, burning his palms.

Wally began climbing upward again. But when he finally reached the upstairs window and got out his knife to unscrew the first screw, he discovered that the Onts had replaced all the screws with bolts!

His Swiss Army knife was not equipped to deal with bolts.

Maybe it was stupid to try to do this alone. Commando fantasies or no, maybe the best plan was to go back to the Spydelles' and get help.

Get the professor and Shirley and even Vampire Dad. Wouldn't giant ants be afraid of a vampire? Better yet, wouldn't giant ants be afraid of a giant *spider*?

Wally climbed down the vines, lowering himself hand over hand. He was sweaty, dirty, and not anxious to be out in Dripping Fang Forest after sunset.

The bugs seemed unusually silent. The only sound was a bird going whip-*poor-WILL*, whip-*poor-WILL*. When Wally heard the snapping of twigs in the underbrush, he decided it was time to get out of there fast. *Cheyenne, I'll be back,* he promised.

CHAPTER 13

The One Thing
You Will Not Do When We
Get to the Spydelles'

The rented yellow school bus carrying Hortense Jolly and the orphans slowed down. Checking the directions she had printed out from MapQuest, Hortense turned on her left turn signal, pulled off the highway under the arch, and looked up at the DRIPPING FANG FOREST signs. At the sign that said trespassers would be ripped open and that their glistening red guts would be strung between the trees like wet laundry. This news was a greater gift to the delighted orphans than an eight-foot-long banana split.

"Could we see glistening red guts strung between trees, Miss Jolly, could we, could we, please?"

"Not now, dear," said Hortense, driving with difficulty along the unpaved road that got progressively narrower and harder to follow.

"When do they rip trespassers open, Miss Jolly? We'd sure like to see *that*."

"I don't think they actually do that, dear. I think that sign was just somebody's idea of a joke. A very *bad* joke, I might add."

The nearly tropical vegetation that surrounded the bus like a dark leafy funnel grew narrower and narrower.

"What do they rip trespassers open *with*, Miss Jolly, scissors? A hatchet? A chain saw?"

"I don't know, dear," said Hortense. The vines scraped the body of the bus and seemed to grasp it like a large leafy hand.

"What are trespassers, Miss Jolly?"

"People who enter private property without permission," said Hortense.

"You mean like us, Miss Jolly? Are we trespassers? Are they going to rip us open and string our glistening red guts between the trees like wet laundry? Are they, huh?"

"Not now," said Hortense. She ground to a stop, set the emergency brake, shut off the engine, and turned around to face her thirty-six passengers. "Okay, listen, orphans, we're on our way to the Spydelles', who are, as I've already told you, the best adopter prospects that I, personally, have ever met. If we can't unload at least a *couple* of you kids on them, it's your own darned fault. Do you all have your song lyrics? Good. Band members, do you all have your instruments and your sheet music? Excellent. Now, Wayne, what is the one thing we have agreed that you will *not* do when we get to the Spydelles'?"

"Set fire to the curtains?" said Wayne.

"Good boy, Wayne. I meant *besides* that. Do you remember?"

"I don't remember."

"We agreed that you would not steal the professor's . . ."

"Teeth?"

"The professor's *watch*, Wayne, the professor's *watch*," said Hortense. "And children, when we see *Mrs.* Spydelle—the enormous spider?—what did we promise we wouldn't do?"

"Barf?" said Orville.

"Thank you, Orville. And what else?"

"Point and scream?"

"Excellent," said Hortense. "Now then, orphans, as we get off the bus, stay together, follow me, and do not lag behind."

The orphans tromped loudly out of the bus.

Observing them through a low hedge was the ten-foot-long giant slug. Although the sun had only recently disappeared below the horizon, it would have been dark enough for the giant slug's glow to be seen if he had not been hiding.

Oho, thought the slug, *what have we here—an entire busload of orphans? Be still, my heart! Two . . . four . . . six . . . eight . . . Holy Toledo, there are thirty-six of them! That's seventy-two succulent feet for a foot-starved slug to nibble on! Sweet suffering chrysanthemums, my cup runneth over! Now then, whose tasty little feet shall I devour first?*

The giant slug looked over the herd and selected little Orville, and pondered a plan to lure him away from the group.

I could flash a bit of my luminescence, he thought, *then ease him off the path and pounce. Ah, I can practically taste those luscious little tootsies now! How shall I serve thee? Let me count the ways: Orphans' Feet Française? Orphans' Feet à la Julia Child? Orphans' Feet au Jus with Lightly Braised Pinkie Toes? Orphans' Feet in a Light Cognac Reduction on a Bed of Baby Toenails? Wait a minute, what's this I sense between this orphan's toes? Mung? Cheesy toe mung? Yecchhh!*

The giant slug's appetite dribbled away like sand through a fist.

Within ten minutes of wandering through Dripping Fang Forest, the orphans discovered that their arms and legs and scalps were covered with tiny multilegged crawly things—and that they were hopelessly lost.

"Which way is the Spydelles' house, Miss Jolly?"

"It's not far from here, children, not far at all."

"But which way is it?"

"I'm not quite sure."

"Are we lost, Miss Jolly?"

"No, no, not lost, children. We just don't know which way we're supposed to be going."

"But isn't that the definition of being lost, Miss Jolly?"

"Please do not be rude, dear. Remember what we do to rude children at the orphanage."

CHAPTER 14

And Now, Please Put Your Hands Together for the One and Only Jolly Days Players!

When Shirley Spydelle opened the door, thirty-six orphan jaws flopped open. Never had they seen anything as disgustingly wonderful in their lives. A larger-than-human-sized spider was better than *yards* of glistening red guts strung between trees like wet wash.

Hortense hit the ground running, speaking so rapidly the words tumbled out faster than she could keep track of them: "I *do* hope we're not interrupting your dinner, Mrs. Spydelle—may I call you Shirley?—but the orphans and I happened to be in the neighborhood and we thought we'd pop in and say hello, just tell me if this is a bad time and we'll be out of here faster than you can say—"

"Well, to tell you the truth—"

"Oh, marvelous, marvelous, I'm *so* glad we aren't interrupting anything important," babbled Hortense. "The kids were wondering if they could have a cold drink, their little throats are so parched and dry, anything at all will do, some water would be perfect, it wouldn't even have to be cold, it could be lukewarm, they wouldn't mind, they can't afford to be choosy because they're orphans and nobody takes their needs very seriously, poor darlings, even me, do you have running water?"

"I could certainly get them some water," said Shirley, "but after that I'm afraid we really—"

"Wonderful, wonderful, and some for me, of course, but with ice cubes? I can't stand water that isn't really *cold,* and in a real *glass* glass, not one of those icky plastic jobs that crack when you squeeze them—that would be so perfect," said Hortense.

"How many of them are there?" Shirley asked.

"The orphans? Oh my, around thirty-six or so, last time I counted, ha-ha, that was a joke, I know there are thirty-six, I don't have to count, and each one sweeter and yummier and more scrumptious than the next, I swear I don't know how I could ever part with even *one* of the little darlings if somebody fell in love with them and wanted to adopt them, but of course I'd have to now, wouldn't I?—are you getting our water, Shirl, or are you just going to stand there, yacking?"

"Oh, I'm sorry," said Shirley. "I'll be right back with the water."

"Come on in, children," said Hortense. "I'm sure Mrs. Spydelle won't mind your being in her house. Watch the door. Did you see all her legs and eyes? Isn't that disgusting? I'm really proud of you children for not pointing or giggling or screaming, just because she's a freak. We have to be *kind* to freaks and treat them like normal people. Now, is everybody ready to do our show? If you don't know the words to the songs by heart, it's perfectly fine to read them off your little cards."

Professor Spydelle entered from his laboratory, wearing his white lab coat.

"Oh, my word," said the professor in his charming British accent. "I *thought* I heard voices out here."

"Hello there, Professor Spydelle," said Hortense. "Children, you remember Professor Spydelle, the gentleman who came to adopt some orphans but was too wishy-washy to make a choice? Just teasing, Professor. I know we just had too many wonderful children for you to do that."

"Yes, yes, that's it," said the professor, "too many wonderful children to make a choice, quite so. What brings you to DFF?"

"DFF?"

"Dripping Fang Forest," said the professor. "Sorry."

"Well, we happened to be in the neighborhood and . . ."

"Really?" said the professor. "I hadn't realized there *was* anything in the neighborhood."

"And we also wanted you to be the very first to hear some exciting new songs that we've written about being an orphan that the children have been rehearsing."

"Ah," said the professor, "how absolutely smashing."

Shirley entered, carrying thirty-seven glasses of water in her many hands.

"Hi, Mrs. Spider," said a little girl named Lou Ann. "That looks like a lot of water to be carrying. If I was your kid, I could help you carry some of it."

"Oh," said Shirley, "well, thank you very much, dear. Edgar, where are Wally and Cheyenne?"

"I haven't the foggiest, my sweet," said Edgar. "I dropped them off at the FBI on the way to work this morning, and I haven't seen them since. I'm sure they'll be along any minute now. Did you know we're to be treated to some exciting new songs about being an orphan that the children have been rehearsing?"

"How perfectly . . . interesting," said Shirley, putting down the glasses of water. "I guess that explains the bongo drums, the ukulele, and the tuba."

"Yes," said Hortense. "And now, without further ado, may I present the Jolly Days Players! Our first song, lady and gentleman, attempts to answer the musical question that so many would-be adopters ask themselves: 'Is It Hard to House an Orphan?' Professor, we dedicate this song to *you*."

Hortense raised a pitch pipe to her lips and blew a harmonica-like note. Then she pointed to the three orphans with the tuba, the ukulele, and the bongo drums. With Hortense Jolly marking time, the band began to play. One by one a series of orphans with surprisingly strong voices each sang a line of the following song:

"Is it hard to <u>house</u> an orphan?" You might ask,
    my dear professor.
"No, it's not, because we'd sleep inside a big
    drawer in your dresser."
"Is it hard to <u>feed</u> an orphan—do you wonder if
    you're able?"
"Well, don't sweat it, 'cause we'd eat the scraps
    that fall right off your table."
"Then it must be hard to <u>clothe</u> an orphan—
    surely <u>that</u> is true?"
"No, it's not, because a blanket or a flour sack
    would do."
"Is it hard to <u>love</u> an orphan—are they awfully
    tough to please?"
"No, they're thrilled to get your smallest smile,
    your very slightest squeeze."

If a cloud should cross our sky, it's just a puffy
    little cirrus.
If we cry, it's in a corner where no one can see
    or hear us.
We swear to you that we would rather die than
    be a bother.

And all we want is just to find another mom or
　　father.
If you had doubts, we hope that we provided you
　　with answers.
'Cause orphans are less trouble than most
　　budgies, mice, or hamsters.

The orphans repeated the chorus together, and the band accompanied them to a big finish:

If you had doubts, we hope that we provided you
　　with answers.
'Cause orphans are less trouble than most
　　budgies, mice, or hamsters.

Shirley clapped politely and hoped the show was over. Edgar clapped a little too loudly. "Smashing!" he said. "Absolutely smashing!"

"Thank you," said Hortense. "Our next number we address to *you*, dear Shirley. We call it 'Could We Love a Spider Mommy?'"

Hortense blew her pitch pipe, the band

began to play, and the kids sang their next song directly to Shirley:

Could we love a spider mommy? Yes, we could.
We don't care if she is weird, if she is good.
  We don't mind if she is buggy,
  As long as she is huggy.
We could love one who lays eggs or who eats
  wood.

Could we love a spider mommy? What's the fuss?
Some are prejudiced against them, but not us.
  With eight arms she'd hold us tight.
  We just hope a careless bite . . .
Won't swell up, turn red, then black, and fill
  with pus.

Could we love a spider mommy? Hey, why <u>not</u>,
  dear?
A lot of choices isn't what we've <u>got</u> here.
  They say beggars can't be choosers.
  And we orphans are such losers,
We need to find a mom fast, or we'll <u>rot</u> here.

Could we love a spider mommy? That depends.
Does she have dung beetles and tarantulas as
friends?
  Or other vermin who might shock us,
  Like flesh-eating streptococcus?
If not, we'd be her kids when this show ends.

When this song was finished, the professor again applauded too loudly. But Shirley's applause seemed a little more sincere.

"And now for a few orphan close-ups," said Hortense. "Tell me, Wayne, why do you want to find someone to adopt you?"

"I happen to know what loneliness is," said Wayne with a crazed leer. He was reading off an index card, half hidden in his pocket. "Mine is a deep black bottomless well, a void that threatens to swallow me daily. The only way I know to cure my own loneliness is to fill a similar void in the life of a parent—or parents—who longs to have a tiny someone to adore him, or her—or them—as the case may be."

"Nicely put," said Hortense.

"I agree," said Edgar. "Quite touching, actually."

"Orville, why do *you* want to find someone to adopt you?" Hortense asked.

"I'm looking for a role model," said Orville in a high, squeaky voice. He was a small child with soft teeth, a bad smell, and dark circles under his eyes. He was reading off notes printed on his hand in ballpoint ink. "Some wonderful adult whom I could look up to, pattern myself after, and devote my life to. I have always yearned to find someone strange and mysterious, perhaps somebody who did not even look human, perhaps—I'm not sure why—someone who had more than the usual number of arms or legs, but I never knew whether such a person even existed."

Edgar turned to Shirley. "What an extraordinary coincidence, my love," he said.

"Thank you, Orville," said Hortense. "Ellie Mae?"

"I am Ellie Mae," said a girl with sores on her face. She was wearing an old laundry bag for a dress and trying to look like she wasn't reading off a tiny scrap of paper. "I'm so desperate to be adopted that tears never stop streaming down my cheeks. And yet I am also a happy, bubbly, almost giddy person. I am never sick and I'm also imp— . . . imperv— . . . What is that word?"

"*Im*-per-*vi-ous*," snapped Hortense under her breath.

". . . *im*-per-*vi-ous* to pain. I had my tonsils removed without anes— . . . anesthe— . . ."

"*An-es*-the-*sia*," snapped Hortense.

". . . *an-es*-the-*sia* as I watched the Cartoon Channel. While toasting s'mores at a recent Jolly Days campfire, my hand caught fire, but I didn't bother blowing it out until my marshmallow had melted into the chocolate."

Edgar and Shirley were by then both sniffling, and Edgar was sobbing openly.

"Well, Professor and Mrs. Spydelle," said Hortense with a triumphant smile, "it seems our tragic little orphans have stirred something deep within you. Would I be correct in thinking that you're willing to bring a little bit of sunshine

into my poor darlings' otherwise cloudy lives by finding a home for them in your hearts?"

Both Edgar and Shirley nodded, stifling sobs.

"There are thirty-six stories at Jolly Days," said Hortense soothingly, "each more heartbreaking than the next, but which of those you've already seen can we ink onto a contract? Little Wayne? Little Orville? Little Ellie Mae? Or what about all three of them? I hate to break up a set."

Edgar and Shirley wiped their noses, as Shirley pulled some contracts out of her purse. She handed one to Wayne and nodded toward the professor. Wayne gave the contract to Edgar and then stole his pen.

"Wayne," said Hortense, controlling her voice with difficulty, "what did we agree before we came here today?"

"Not to steal his watch," said Wayne.

"Give back his pen," said Hortense between tightly clenched teeth. Wayne stuck out his tongue, then gave back the professor's pen.

"Good boy, Wayne," said Hortense. "See how nicely he gave it back? Thank you, Wayne."

"No problem," said Wayne.

"That was quite remarkable, how quickly he gave it back," said the professor, dabbing at his eyes. "Did you see that, Shirley?"

Shirley looked at her husband.

A very bad smell was coming in waves from Orville's direction.

"Miss Jolly," Orville whispered, "I have a secret to tell you."

"I don't think it's a secret anymore, Orville," said Hortense Jolly with a sigh.

"I'm sorry, Miss Jolly," Orville whispered.

"That's all right, dear," said Hortense. "I guess we're all a little excited tonight, even me."

"Oh, did you poo in your pants, too, Miss Jolly?" Orville whispered.

That was the point at which Ellie Mae threw up her lunch.

Hortense managed a weak smile. *We almost had them,* she thought, *we had them—right up to the pen stealing, the poop, and the puke. So close, so heartbreakingly close!*

The professor and Shirley seemed to have recovered their composure. Dabbing at six of her eight eyes, Shirley was the first to speak.

"Miss Jolly, Edgar and I were very moved by your orphans' stories, very moved. But, well, I think we just need some time to think about all of this."

"I don't think we need that much time, actually," said Edgar.

"Take all the time you need," said Hortense, misunderstanding the professor. She briefly considered and then decided against a last-ditch try at closing the sale by offering them a special one-time-only, three-for-the-price-of-one deal. "Come, children," she said instead, "it's time we got back to the orphanage."

That was when Wally burst in the door.

"Guys," he announced, "Cheyenne has been captured by the Onts! They're starving her, and I'm not sure what else they're going to do!

But if we all go over there now, I think we can rescue her and save her life! Who's coming with me?"

Everyone was momentarily stunned by Wally's announcement.

"I'll join you," said Shirley. "I think I can handle at least one of those giant ants."

"My word," said Edgar. "I'll join you, too. I believe I could hurl toxic chemicals from my laboratory at them. It would be fascinating to see how ants that size defend themselves."

"I'm in, too," said Rocco, the bully. "I'd love to kick some ant butt!"

"I could set fire to their house!" said Wayne with a crazed smile.

"I could poo on their carpet!" said Orville. "Do they have a carpet?"

The rest of the orphans gave excited suggestions about what they each could do. Hortense Jolly raised her hand for silence. Then, in a voice quavering with emotion, she said, "Cheyenne is very dear to me. I would be honored to help whoop the Mandible sisters' sorry behinds and save her!"

Everybody cheered. Then Vampire Dad came in.

"What's everybody cheering about?" he asked.

"Dad, Cheyenne's been captured by the Onts," said Wally. "We're all going over to Mandible House now to try and save her. Will you join us?"

"Oh, my poor little girl!" he cried. "Yes, Wally, of *course* I'll join you! And we shall see how they handle a vampire's wrath!"

The orphans couldn't believe their ears.

"You're a *vampire*?" asked Rocco.

In reply Dad merely opened his mouth, flashed his fangs, and unfurled his large leathery wings.

The orphans squealed like kids on a roller coaster.

CHAPTER 15

We're Looking for a Few Good Men—Also Some Wolves and Maybe a Giant Slug

Because it was then quite dark and everyone was a little scared to be out in Dripping Fang Forest, Edgar used toxic chemicals from his lab to make each of them a torch, which they all lit as soon as they went outside. The flaming torches snapped and crackled and cast intriguing shadows. With all that fire and all that company, it didn't seem quite so scary.

A light breeze carried the pungent smells of moist earth and pine. A cottony blanket of fog covered the ground, making it difficult to see one's feet. Crickets *kreek*ed in the underbrush.

Armies of insects rubbed their legs together in unison, sounding like the percussion section of a Mexican band. The night bugs made a louder racket than usual, as if they sensed that something big was about to happen. Through the trees could be seen occasional flashes of lightning. Far away, thunder grumbled.

Wally, Dad, Edgar, Shirley, Hortense, and the thirty-six orphans hadn't gone more than half a mile before they saw something ahead of them that looked like glowing red coals floating in the air. Then they heard the growling, and they realized the glowing red coals were eyes. Soon they were surrounded by wolves.

Wally recognized Fred, the leader, from the night he and Cheyenne had stood up to the entire pack and outbluffed them.

"Hey, Fred," said Wally. "Hey there, wolf-pack guys!"

"Hey," Fred answered with little enthusiasm.

"So, how you guys doing?" asked Wally.

"Not too bad," said Fred. "You know."

"Boy, am I ever glad I ran into you!" said

Wally. "Oh, by the way, guys, this is my dad, Sheldon Shluffmuffin, and I think you already know Professor Spydelle and his wife, Shirley? That's Hortense Jolly over there, the owner of the Jolly Days Orphanage, and those are the orphans."

Everybody muttered the usual polite hellos. The orphans whispered and pointed at the wolves, and were very impressed.

"So, Fred," Wally continued, "you remember my sister, Cheyenne, right? Well, she's been captured by the giant ants who live farther down the path at Mandible House. They're planning to starve her. If we don't get her out of there soon, she's dead. The poor little kid is only ten. So we're going over to Mandible House now. We're going to surround the place and rescue Cheyenne. It would be so cool if you guys could join us. What do you say?"

Fred looked at Wally, then shook his head in disbelief.

"Boy, have *you* ever got the wrong guys," said Fred.

"What?" said Wally.

"I don't know who you think you're talking to, man," said Fred. "Maybe you see us as this lovable band of ruffians who can be urged into cheerful self-sacrifice by a cheesy plea for help? Well, you're mistaken."

"We're vicious predators, pal," said another wolf, "not wimpy do-gooders. We're not moved by your sister's plight, nor by your cheap guilt-inducing attempt to save her."

"Plus which," said Fred, "I seem to recall an incident not long ago in which you bit me on the nose and your sister threw pepper in my face."

"Right," said Wally. "So I'm guessing that would be a no?"

"You're guessing correctly," said Fred. "And maybe you wouldn't be acting so cocky if you weren't with all of your friends."

"Really?" said Wally. "I wasn't with all of my friends the *last* time—it was just me and Cheyenne against you and your whole wolf pack. And as soon as we stood up to you, you guys all took off and went home."

Fred glared at Wally, then began a low growl deep in his chest.

Wally began to growl as well.

"All right," said Fred, "there's no need to get grouchy about it." He turned and trotted away. The members of the pack loped off after him.

The orphans applauded Wally and pounded him on the back.

Wally and the gang continued down the path toward Mandible House. The flashes of lightning appeared more frequently through the trees. The answering grumbles of thunder followed faster and louder. It sounded like next-door neighbors throwing furniture downstairs. A wind with some chill in it began to blow, shaking the treetops.

"Looks like we might be getting a storm soon," said Shirley.

"Cool. We can kick ant butt in the rain," said Rocco.

Wally spotted something glowing about twenty yards ahead of them in the underbrush. It was nearly ten feet long. It was the giant slug.

"Hey there, Sluggo!" called Wally, wondering if he might be pushing things by making up a nickname. "Haven't seen *you* since the night my sister and I escaped from the Mandibles! Speaking of my sister, she's been captured by the giant ants, and we're all going over to Mandible House now to try and rescue her. Want to join us?"

"Why must it always be about *you*?" said the giant slug.

"Excuse me?" said Wally.

"Why is it never about *me*?" said the slug. "What about *my* needs? Am I not entitled to have needs?"

"I'm sorry," said Wally. "I didn't think—"

"That's just the trouble," said the giant slug, "you didn't *think*. And wasn't Cheyenne the young lady who poured the contents of a salt-shaker on me that night?"

"Uh, she might have done a tiny bit of salt pouring that night," said Wally. "She was pretty upset about the giant ants, and then, of course, you were trying to chow down on her foot, so . . ."

"For your information," said the slug, "getting salt poured on oneself really smarts if one happens to be a slug. It smarts and it leaves nasty little scars that need to be removed by an expensive laser process. So, thanks for the invitation, but I'm afraid I'm *not* going to join you and your tacky torch-wielding lynch mob."

"Okay," said Wally.

"And please don't contact me again," said the slug, "unless it's to join a mob pouring salt on Cheyenne!"

CHAPTER 16

Fall of the House of Mandible

Flickering torches held high, Wally, Dad, Edgar, Shirley, Hortense Jolly, and the orphans surrounded Mandible House. There was incredible energy and excitement in the air. None of them had ever taken part in something this heroic before. Saving someone's life and kicking the butts of monsters was the stuff of action movies and video games. And it was positively thrilling to be part of a mob.

The lightning flashes and thunder crashes were very close together, and the wind howled through the trees. Every few seconds there was a spattering of raindrops.

"I wonder if they even know we're out here," said Ellie Mae.

"You kidding me?" said Rocco. "With all these torches? How could they *not* know?"

"I so hope they haven't harmed Cheyenne yet," said Shirley.

"Do you think they'll put up much of a fight?" asked Hortense nervously.

"Of course they will," said Wally. "But we outnumber them twenty-to-one."

"I pray nobody gets killed," said Shirley.

"Well, in any conflict this size you've got to expect a *few* fatalities," said Wally carelessly, as though he were a veteran of many conflicts like this.

"I'm ready to kick butts and bite necks," said Vampire Dad.

"I'm ready to give them a pretty good scare," said Shirley.

"Are you prepared to use *your* fangs, Shirley?" Wally asked.

"Oh, dear me," said Shirley, "do you really think that will be necessary?"

There seemed to be no activity inside Mandible House. There didn't seem to be any lights in the windows. The old Gothic mansion stared down at them with dead eyes.

"I say, Wally," said the professor, "the windows appear to be dark. Do you think that's a defensive measure?"

"Absolutely," said Wally. "They turned off the lights the minute they heard us coming. You don't want to make yourself a target by keeping your house lit. They're watching us from those darkened windows now, realizing they're trapped and wondering what we're going to do next."

"What *are* we going to do next, Wally?" asked the professor.

"Am I in charge?" Wally asked, excited by the idea.

"Well, it does seem to be your show," said the professor.

"Wow," said Wally, suddenly dizzy with power. He thought a moment, then knew what they could try. "Okay, gang, here's what we'll do. First, let's all put out our torches. Just shove them in the dirt and they'll go out. Good. Next, we're going to enter the house. I've seen this a million times in movies. Shirley, Edgar, Dad, and I will go in the first wave. Then Hortense will bring in the orphans to mop up."

More flashes of lightning. More explosions of thunder. More raindrops.

"What do we do when we see them?" asked Shirley.

"Shirley, you'll scare the heck out of them. Edgar will throw his toxic chemicals at them. Dad will bite them, and I'll ... punch them in the stomach or something. Everybody ready?"

There were cries of "Yes!" and "Ready!" and "Let's roll!"

"All right, gang, on my signal ..."

Wally crept up to the front door and slowly turned the knob. The door didn't open.

"This door is locked," said Wally. "Darn!"

"Most people do tend to lock their doors these days," said Hortense dryly.

"I think I can help you with that, son," said Vampire Dad. He sprang to the front door, knelt down before it, and licked the lock with his long red vampire tongue.

The orphans *ooh*ed, the lock tumblers clicked, and the door snapped open.

Wally gave the arm signal of all commando leaders and heads of SWAT teams, and then entered the house, followed by Dad, Edgar, Shirley, Hortense, and the orphans. Outside it had begun to rain in earnest.

Wally's heart was hammering so hard in his chest, he thought it would crack a rib. He could hardly breathe from excitement.

"Sssshhh," he said, although nobody had made a sound.

The house was dark and still. There was a strong coppery odor and the smell of floor wax. From somewhere below came an ominous sound: *Ch-ch-ch-ch-ch* . . . The sound of the slimy super-larvae.

Somewhere close by, the giant ants were watching, listening, biding their time—ready to pounce, ready to sink their terrible ant jaws into soft human flesh.

Well, thought Wally, *our team has a few terrible jaws of our own, and we're the good guys, so bring it on!*

They all waited in the hallway, holding their breaths, for the enemy to strike. Nothing happened.

Prickly sensations ran up Wally's back between his shoulder blades. His scalp began to sweat. Nothing happened.

A floorboard creaked, and Wally spun around, ready to punch somebody in the stomach, but it was only Shirley, standing just behind him.

"Wally," Shirley whispered, "there's nobody here."

"What do you mean?" Wally whispered. "How do you know that?"

"I can sense these things," said Shirley. "I'm a spider. Trust me, there's nobody here."

She crept to the electric switch on the wall and flicked it on. The sudden bright light made Wally squint, but Shirley was right. There was nobody home.

Wally had been ready to fight, to punch insects in the stomach, to die if necessary. He had not expected to find...nobody home. It was disappointing, it was anticlimactic, and SWAT team commander Wally didn't know what to do next.

CHAPTER 17

Get Your Free Flu Virus—
Only One to a Customer, Please

In the cosmetics section of a department store in downtown Cincinnati, Dagmar, Hedy, and Cheyenne were busily at work. Wearing their distinctive black hats, black sunglasses, and full-length black gloves, they sprayed startled customers from perfume atomizers filled with flu virus bought from a gnome in the musical instruments shop. A frowning woman in horn-rimmed glasses and a no-nonsense striped suit hurried over.

"May I ask what you're doing?" she demanded.

"Giving out free samples of a new fragrance," said Dagmar. "Chanel Number Two."

"And who gave you permission to do this?" the woman demanded.

"Permission?" said Dagmar. "Why would we need permission to give out free samples?"

"If you leave immediately, I won't have you thrown out," said the frowning woman.

"But we have only begun to give out our samples, dear," said Hedy.

"Immediately, or I'll have you arrested," said the woman.

Realizing they could infect more people outside, anyway, Dagmar allowed Hedy, Cheyenne, and herself to be ushered out of the department store and into the street.

Traffic swarmed and blared on all sides of them. There were flashes of lightning.

"Well, *that* was unpleasant," said Cheyenne.

"The nerve of that woman," said Hedy.

"I gave her a spray right in the face, Ont Hedy," said Cheyenne, wiping her nose.

"Good girl," said Hedy. "Well, Dagmar, what do you suggest we do now?"

"Look around you," said Dagmar. "What do you see?"

Hedy and Cheyenne looked around.

"Cars, buses, trucks, humans coming home from work," said Hedy.

"Hundreds of happy people going to cozy homes to have dinner with their loving families," said Cheyenne.

"You know what *I* see?" said Dagmar. "Hundreds of humans eager to inhale our flu virus so that we may harvest their snot to feed our hungry babies. Ladies, resume your spraying!"

With new enthusiasm, Dagmar, Hedy, and Cheyenne resumed their spraying.

"Hey, get that out of my face!" said a man carrying an attaché case. "What *is* that stuff?"

"Breath spray," said Cheyenne. "We're trying to stamp out an epidemic of halitosis."

"Breath spray?" said the man. "But you're just spraying it into the air."

"Did she say *breath* spray?" asked Dagmar. "She meant *death* spray—to kill the West Nile mosquito virus."

"Oh," said the man. "Well, why didn't you say so?"

CHAPTER 18

And Now, Back to the Fall

Wally, Dad, Edgar, Shirley, Hortense, and the orphans searched the house. Just to be on the safe side, they examined every room, including upstairs bedrooms, bathrooms, and closets. Shirley was right; there was nobody home.

Then Wally took them down into the creepy cellar. They sloshed through the two inches of standing water on the floor, and he showed them the machines that converted snot and foot stink into nourishment for the larvae. The orphans loved the Snot Press and the Odor Extractor. Then he showed them the larvae themselves. The orphans gagged. Everyone found the slimy babies gross and disgusting. Everyone, that is, but Shirley.

"You have to admit they're kind of cute," she said, smiling.

"What should we do with them?" Wally asked. "I mean, we really ought to destroy them now that we have the chance, but how?"

"They're coming back!" said Shirley suddenly. "The Mandible sisters are coming back. And Cheyenne is with them."

"How do you know?" Wally asked.

"I sense them," said Shirley. "Trust me, okay?"

"Turn out all the lights!" said Wally. "Upstairs, too! Everybody hide!"

"This isn't going to work," said Shirley. "Ants have an incredible sense of smell. They'll be able to smell us, especially these stinky orphans. We'll have to hide the orphans somewhere so they can't be smelled as easily."

"You mean like Europe?" said Wally. "Okay, listen. The orphans stay down here in the cellar

127

with Miss Jolly. Dad, Shirley, Edgar, and I will go upstairs and hide in the hallway. Quick!"

Wally, Dad, Shirley, and Edgar scrambled upstairs, closing the cellar door securely on Hortense and the orphans. They turned off all the lights and held their breaths.

A few minutes later they heard the front door being unlocked. The door creaked inward. The rain had stopped, but the lightning and thunder continued.

"Cheyenne, go in and turn on the lights," called Dagmar. "You know I hate to enter a dark house."

Cheyenne walked in cautiously and headed toward the light switch on the wall.

"*Pssstt,*" Wally whispered. "Cheyenne, it's me, Wally!"

"Wally? But how did you ever...?"

"*Sssshhh!*" Wally whispered. "I came back, just as I promised, and I brought help—Dad, Shirley, the professor, Miss Jolly, and the orphans. You can come back with me now and leave this horrible place forever!"

"Oh wow," said Cheyenne, stifling a sneeze. "That's so cool, Wally. I can't believe you did this. Uh, when is it you want me to leave, exactly?"

"What do you mean?" Wally whispered.

"Well, because I'm going to need a little time to, like, you know, get packed and say good-bye and stuff."

"'Say *good-bye*'?" Wally repeated. "Cheyenne, the Mandibles *kidnapped* you. You weren't their houseguest, you were their *prisoner.* They were your *captors.* Prisoners don't have to say good-bye to their *captors.*"

"Well, *I* know that, Wally," said Cheyenne. "But there's such a thing as being nice, and then there's such a thing as being rude."

Outside there was a loud crash of thunder.

"Cheyenne!" called Dagmar. "Why haven't you turned on the lights? Can't you find them?"

"Uh, not yet, Ont Dagmar!" called Cheyenne. "I'm having a little trouble locating them in the dark!"

"They're on the wall on the right, just as you enter!" called Dagmar. "Hurry up!"

"Okay, Ont Dagmar!" Cheyenne called.

"You know something?" Wally whispered. "You don't seem as grateful to be rescued as I thought you'd be."

"Oh no, no, please don't get me wrong," said Cheyenne. "I think getting rescued is really cool, Wally. Really, really, incredibly cool, and so sweet and brave of you to do. It's just that I didn't know you were going to come for me so *soon*, okay? And I kind of made other plans and everything, with Hedy and stuff. Not that they couldn't be changed, I mean, but still."

"Somebody's here!" shouted Dagmar. "I smell the stink of human children! *Many* human children! *Who is in my house?*"

As Dagmar and Hedy entered the house, Wally snapped on the lights.

The instant the lights came on, Dad bared his fangs. Dagmar and Hedy froze.

"What the . . . ?" said Dagmar.

Edgar held up two glass vials for the Mandibles to see. They were filled with bright blue liquid that glowed like the flame of a gas stove. He threw one at each of the giant ants. Wherever the toxic liquid hit them, it steamed and sizzled and burned through their clothing like acid.

Instantly, Shirley reared up on her hind legs in the spider's traditional fighting position.

With a shriek so high-pitched that Wally almost couldn't hear it, Dagmar and Hedy backed away from Shirley.

The Onts dropped to all sixes and scrambled for the cellar door. They tore it open and scuttled down the stairs.

"Now!" shouted Hortense.

The orphans began throwing things they'd found in the basement at the Onts—hammers, hatchets, hoses, rakes, saws, shovels, rusty garden tools, cans of Chef Boyardee spaghetti, and anything else they could get their hands on.

Heavy tools hit the Snot Press and the Odor Extractor, which fell over and knocked Dagmar and Hedy unconscious. The falling Snot Press and Odor Extractor also upset a tank of gasoline and threw dozens of larvae out of their cocoons. The hungry larvae feasted upon the unconscious bodies of their guardians.

The gasoline from the upset tank floated on the water that covered the basement floor, forming transparent rainbow-colored swirls. Then it ignited from the flames in the furnace with a fiery *whoosh!* Hundreds of larvae were consumed by the flames, screaming *"Ch-ch-ch-ch-ch!"* as they perished.

The twins, Vampire Dad, the Spydelles, Hortense Jolly, and the orphans fled up the cellar steps and stampeded outside.

Unnoticed by everyone, something large and on fire crept painfully to the cellar wall, loosened a metal grate, and crawled into an air shaft.

"We did it!" Wally yelled. "We killed them!"

"We kicked their butts!" Rocco shouted. "Yee-ha!"

"I threw spaghetti at them!" Orville screamed. "I pooed my pants, too, Miss Jolly, but I don't even care!"

"Neither do I, Orville," said Hortense wearily. "Neither do I."

"We're burning their whole house down," said Wayne, his eyes glinting crazily in the flames. "How beautiful!"

"How ghastly!" said Shirley, staring at the

fire, her eyes streaming with tears. "How perfectly ghastly!"

"It may be ghastly, dear," said Edgar softly, "but they were trying to destroy the human race."

"Maybe so," said Shirley, "but nobody deserves to die that way."

It had started to rain again, but not enough to dampen the fire. Mandible House was now engulfed. Tongues of bright orange flame licked at the wooden shingled skin that covered the skeleton of the ancient structure as if it were a Mister Softee ice-cream cone. The heat was so intense on the faces of those watching the fire, they felt they were getting a bad sunburn.

"Move back, kids!" Dad warned. It began to rain harder. Dad wrapped his leathery wings lovingly around Wally and Cheyenne to shield them from the downpour. If his wings disturbed them, they didn't show it.

"Maybe we should have called the fire department or something," said Cheyenne.

"There is no fire department in Dripping

Fang Forest," said Edgar, "not even a volunteer operation. The closest fire department is in Cincinnati, which is more than an hour away."

"They would never have come all the way out here, honey," said Dad.

"I guess you're right," said Cheyenne. She blew her nose loudly into a Kleenex, but there was no longer anybody to snatch it out of her hands.

When the fire was at its very hottest, the skies exploded in light and sound. A bolt of lightning streaked down and struck Mandible House. Everybody gasped. There was an unearthly cracking sound. The House of Mandible fell inward upon itself, and crumbled to the ground in slow motion. A million sparklers flew upward as it crashed.

Cheyenne seemed frozen. She stared at the smoking pile of red-hot rubble that had once been Mandible House. The slanting rain made the rubble hiss like a pile of pythons.

"How are you feeling now, Cheyenne?" Edgar asked.

"I don't know," said Cheyenne. "I mean, it's so awful that Hedy, Dagmar, and the babies had to die like that."

"Hedy and Dagmar were giant ants who tried to kill us," said Wally. "The babies were disgusting super-larvae that were going to replace mankind and end life on Earth as we know it."

"I know that, Wally," said Cheyenne sadly. "But Hedy was nice to me. Even Dagmar had her good points."

Edgar poured tobacco into his pipe and touched a match to the bowl. The rain guaranteed the pipe would not stay lit.

"I believe what we're seeing here in Cheyenne is a textbook example of the Stockholm syndrome," he said.

"Is that when kidnap victims become friendly with their captors?" Shirley asked.

"Precisely, my pet," said the professor, puffing repeatedly to try to light the tobacco. "They're overly impressed by small acts of kindness on the part of their captors and they begin to identify with them. The name comes from a 1973 hostage crisis at a bank in Stockholm, Sweden. A year later, in 1974, billionaire newspaper heiress Patty Hearst was captured in this country by a radical political group—the Symbionese Liberation Army, I believe they called themselves. Miss Hearst, who'd renamed herself Tania, eventually helped them rob a bank."

"I never would have helped them rob a bank," said Cheyenne.

CHAPTER 19

The Mother of Us All

Somewhere deep in Dripping Fang Forest, fifty feet below the surface, in a huge dimly lit underground cavern, something vast, obese, and disgusting lay slumbering. It was more than ninety feet long, the size of a blue whale.

Someone awakened the disgustingly obese creature very apologetically.

"Your Highness, Mother of Mothers," said the awakener, "I beg you to forgive the intrusion, but I thought you should hear this immediately. A visitor has arrived with dreadful news."

The whale-sized creature was the Ont Queen, Absolute Ruler for Life of All Giant Onts in Ohio. She shifted slightly and squinted to look down the length of her ninety-foot body to see the visitor at her feet.

"Pray tell, visitor, what is this dreadful news you bring?" said the Ont Queen.

"Your Highness, Dagmar Mandible is dead! The House of Mandible has fallen and been consumed by flames, and the Shluffmuffin twins have prevailed!" said the visitor with a sob.

The visitor was badly burned and hideously disfigured. She shook with emotion.

"Who brings such dreadful news, and why should we believe you?" demanded the Ont Queen.

The Ont Queen was dressed in a silk gown large enough to contain an office building. She was surrounded by dozens of worker and soldier onts. The soldiers wore camouflage fatigues and GI boots. The underground cavern itself was entirely plated in twenty-four-carat gold. Even the stalactites and stalagmites were gold.

"Your Highness, do not doubt my news," said the visitor. "I am Hedy Mandible."

At these words the Ont Queen grew livid.

"Cincinnati's snot must be harvested for the babies!" she shouted. "The destruction of the House of Mandible must be avenged! And the Shluffmuffin twins must be assassinated!"

"Your Highness, Queen of Queens, Mother of Mothers," said Hedy, "Cheyenne Shluffmuffin has been hypnotized and given a posthypnotic suggestion that can be triggered by a signal I implanted in her subconscious mind. She could be extremely useful in our master plan to replace mankind and end life on Earth as we know it."

"In that case," declared the Ont Queen in her most regal voice, "the life of Cheyenne Shluffmuffin will be spared. But Walter Shluffmuffin shall surely die!"

What's Next for the Shluffmuffin Twins?

Did that horrible fire in Mandible House spell the end of the dreaded Mandible sisters? If so, who was the large flaming creature that crept painfully to the cellar wall, loosened a metal grate, and crawled into an air shaft?

Okay, it was Hedy Mandible, the nicer of the two ont sisters. But how nice is she going to be, now that she's been hideously disfigured by that fire? Don't you think she's going to be a tad bitter toward the people who destroyed her house, and burned her beloved sister and their precious ont babies to a crisp?

And who the heck is that gross whale-sized Ont Queen we've just met? How many soldier onts does she have, and how many thousands of giant ont larvae is she breeding in her sinister underground fortress? How does she plan to use poor hypnotically controlled Cheyenne against her own family and friends? Does she *really* plan to have Wally killed? And if so, what sick method will she use—and how could Wally possibly escape? More important, doesn't her very existence threaten every human being in the state of Ohio?

Even if you're not living in Ohio—even if you're several states away, calmly reading this book—what makes you think you're not in imminent danger of being enslaved by giant onts yourself, onts who are even now living underground in your very own neighborhood, plotting to knock on your door one night and grab you—grotesque creatures with huge eyes, creepy antennae, ghastly mandibles that look like gigantic sideways black pliers dripping with slime, and with more legs than your whole entire family combined?

You seriously can*not* afford to miss the Shluffmuffins' next hair-raising, heart-racing, nausea-inducing adventure—Secrets of Dripping Fang, Book Five: *The Shluffmuffin Boy Is History*! Seriously, you can't.

DAN GREENBURG writes the popular Zack Files series for kids and has also written many bestselling books for grown-ups. His sixty-six books have been translated into twenty languages. To research his writing, Dan has worked with N.Y. firefighters and homicide cops, searched for the Loch Ness monster, flown upside down in an open-cockpit plane, taken part in voodoo ceremonies in Haiti, and disciplined tigers on a Texas ranch. He has not, however, personally encountered any zombies or vampires—at least not yet. Dan lives north of New York with wife Judith, son Zack, and many cats.

SCOTT M. FISCHER glided through high school doing extra-credit art assignments for math teachers, which is kinda boring stuff to draw. Next he went to art school, where he learned to paint even more boring things—like flower vases. However, he swears that since then he has drawn nothing but cool stuff—like oozy, drooling monsters, treacherous villains, and the occasional flower vase . . . that has fangs and eats flowers for breakfast!